Wednesday's Writer

V

A Spanking New Anthology

From the

Todmorden Writers' Group

December 2014

Compiled and Edited by Andy Fraser

ISBN: 978-1-326-09369-3
Published via Lulu.com
1st Edition printed 2014
Copyright © 2014 the Todmorden Writers' Group.
All rights reserved.

All work is the copyright of the individual author and is produced with their explicit permission. Anyone wishing to use any material in this anthology should contact the editor at fraserai@yahoo.com

Contents

Introduction 5
Midsummer's Night 8
Le Tour Comes to the Calder Valley............................10
Dreams 13
The Forgotten War 16
Another Place* 19
Psycho-Active Strepsil..21
Seaside Town in the Rain 26
Indian Summer..28
Visit Me 30
The Ballad of Zaak and Ermaine 36
Remembering David...42
A Pleasure to Burn...45
Late March and they are Still Not Here........................48
Bombability 51
My Daughter's Breathing 56
The Working Dead..59
A Midsummer Night's Dream 68
A Pterodactyl Lacking Charity......................................70
The Race 75
The Contributors 77

Introduction

By *Andy Fraser & Alison Shelton*

Well, this moment was bound to come one day or another. After seven years leading the merry Wednesdays I have been forced, through other commitments, to hand over the reins of power to my successor. Though I admit to being completely unable to bow out gracefully, I only heckle from the back-row now and the newsletters I still send contain only a few bitter jibes per week. In truth, I leave the group in a vibrant state and in very capable hands, so I know everything will be fine. Yet I feel sad not to be at the meetings any longer.

From its humble beginnings in the room above, what is now, the delicious Hanniman Restaurant, this group has blossomed and grown into something I am very proud of, as founder, host and as member. Whenever I find myself in Tod on a Wednesday evening, I'll still be there listening and giving my opinion and who knows what the future might bring.

I know what this year has brought. 2014 has been a good year for the writers' group and, although there is no entry in this anthology from John Clarke, I must single him out for his success at the Contact Theatre and in Manchester's 24:7 drama festival for which he has staged his own plays.

And so it is time to pass the baton onto Alison, the new chairwoman of the Wednesday's Writers. I have to say a huge thank you for everything she has done to support me in the past and everything she has taken on in the future.

Andy Fraser

Introduction

This year, as usual, the fortnightly writers' group membership has ebbed and flowed; with the writers all being creative folk, many are also involved in the local theatre and are occasionally busy doing set design or rehearsals on a Wednesday evening. That said we have also welcomed some new members who have added to the talent pool. It has been noted that, among the longer-standing members, our styles have changed and our writing has got better and better as the years have gone by. In addition, the Wednesday Writers have been actively participating in writing competitions, including two finalists in the Voices of Todmorden; our continued success demonstrating the amazing writing skills in the group.

Our annual anthology is a great source of comparison of the group's creative development year on year and this year, as ever, it has been a difficult task to whittle the writers' work down to this great selection. The themes this year have been as varied and challenging as ever, from 'resurrection' to 'old boots', ensuring that everyone continues to develop their writing and providing some interesting discussion on the night.

If you live in or around Todmorden, the Wednesday's Writers' group is always happy to welcome new members. Whether you're an avid writer looking to develop your skills further or if you want to start writing, come a join our passionate, creative sessions fortnightly on a Wednesday evening from 7.30pm. Contact fraserai@yahoo.com for more information and for the meeting dates.

Alison Shelton
November 2014

Midsummer's Night

Midsummer's Night

by *Christine Holley*

The first time we met on a midsummer night
She smiled at me and I held her tight
We swore we would love till the end of time
I would be hers and she would be mine
But the days grew short and the nights grew long
And it seemed our love was not that strong
Living a life that could not last
Based on happiness in the past
Our dreams began to fade away
Dissolving in the light of day
Gradually we drifted apart
Both seeking love in another's heart
But sometimes when winter is on the wane
I look at the sky and think again
Of how we met on a midsummer night
And she smiled at me and I held her tight

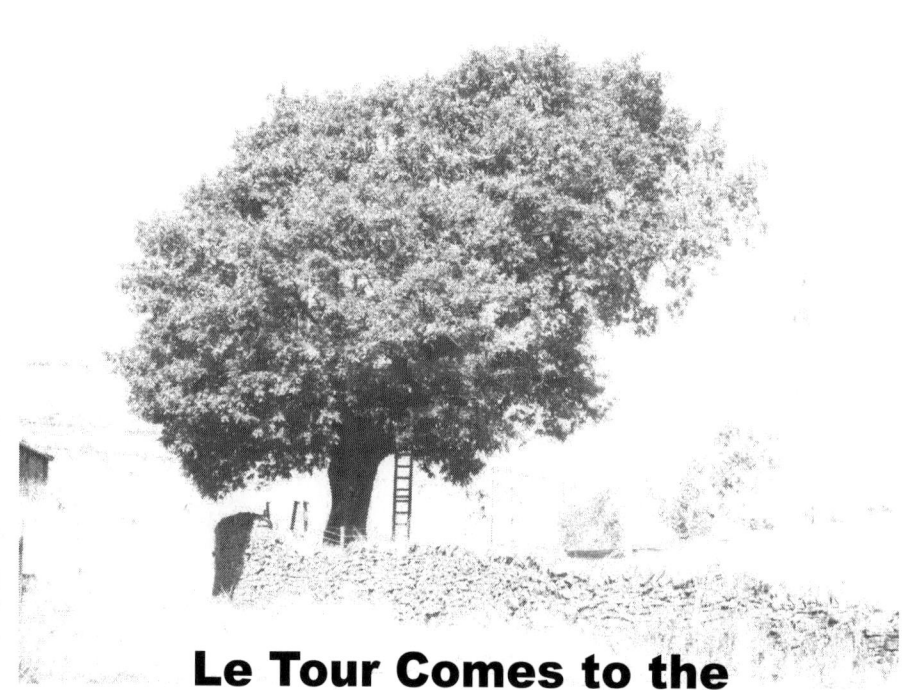

Le Tour Comes to the Calder Valley

Le Tour Comes to the Calder Valley

by *Anthony Peter*

Hey-day and ho-day and jolly high-day holiday,
and along the sunlit canal we walk.
The Aylesburys are fat and goosing the grass
where the gongoozler dawdles his roll-up day
and his Guinness-drinking friend with his fire
against the fence rails stares a substantial
smile soused beside his washing clothed boat.
Look out for canalside cyclists! Ting ting!
Thank you! Allotments heave with beans and spuds,
compost breathes with depths of microbial
Olympics and tangles of tigering brandlings.

The Calder valley's all a-brim with light!

By locks we pause and watch the oaky hangs
of branch and tannined mast, the eye alert
for flitter or flash of sun-buffed breast.
'It's a mile now', the blue-clad lass declares.
We pass the time of uneventful day.
'We fished one out,' she says. 'He over-
balanced and in he went, bike and all, no worse
for wear when we got him out. Panniers
overpacked.' Cheers!

Le Tour Comes to the Calder Valley

At Stubbing Wharf we leave
the tow and cross the road. A wall presents
itself to sit on, so we do. Sarnies:
Brian's big soft teacakes stuffed with tongue
and chicken, a salad lightly salted
and a crunch of lettuce.

Parked cars and open sky,
a thrumless hour as we amble bare-necked
in one o'clock sun towards The Fox and Goose.

Ah! The cool of this lemony cowslip corner
kegged with empties and Trevor's cross-legged welcome;
the quiet of the bar that basks in dimness
lit by beer and brightness. Lycra is pacing
up Howarth over its boneshaking cobbles,
past the Black Bull, and the hushed and vaulted earth
of the Brontes, off towards Oxenhope
Côte, and good luck to them. 'What's a good pint?'
'Try this – "Good Measure".' 'Hmm. Too bitter for me.'
'Then you'll prefer this – it's "Ball Relief."' Hopped
fragrance of summer, fruit on the finish,
suppable buddy for elderflower
cider, the bottle of choice for my Jan.
With three other loungers we slump in the hum
of the pub. The world has deserted us.
We watch on the telly the road unroll
under the wheels of supertrained athletes,
we who are training ourselves
in the art of the elbow and glass. Let be!
This comfortable coterie is pacing
itself into anonymous blitheness
in a world awash with supping and sunlight and smiles.

Dreams

Dreams

by *Cindy Shanks*

'If only I could win the lottery,' Abigail thought glancing at the red sports car, gleaming in the display window.

Visualising her brown hair flowing behind her, designer sunglasses and a Katie Price pout, it was a dream.

'The probability of winning the lottery – for me it's impossible especially when I've hardly any change for a ticket.'

She caught sight of the smooth salesman frowning at her in disbelief and had one quick glance before hurrying past.

Her black shoe heels worn down by concrete and endless job searching, Abigail pulled the shabby jacket closer to her – losing her job was the last thing she needed.

Twelve months ago she'd graduated from her Arts course only to find herself at the front of the job seekers queue, being stared at by someone who still had spots and looked like he was on work experience. With his trendy black glasses, which he kept pushing up his nose, he said,

'You'll have to set your sights lower. How about shelf stacking or maybe waitressing until you find the right position for your - er qualifications? If not, then the government demands you do some worthwhile voluntary work.'

No support, nothing, only the constant reminder she was a nuisance, a dreadful burden and a drain on tax payers. Even worse her husband had left her, unable to understand why she needed to express herself with splashes of colour or why she must find herself at 31 and then end up worse off than when she had started. Six months, or maybe twelve months, she thought arriving at Alessandro's. May be then she'd have to give up on her artistic dream.

'Come on Abigail, people are waiting,' the owner said.

'The probability of having a satisfied customer who tipped... most unlikely. The probability of having a grumpy member of the public... Certain.'

She smiled as she threw herself into orders until the last person left.

Feet aching and a long walk home later, she wondered if anyone would reply to her emails. Job searches, examples of work, commissions, advertising. She'd done everything they'd told her at university. The tiny flat was covered with sketches and paintings to brighten up the dismal surroundings.

A few more months, she thought and then I'll have to enrol on a P.G.C.E. and teach everyone else how to draw or paint. She shuddered. Secondary children.

Exhausted, she almost missed the blinking light on her telephone. Her hands shook as she played the message. Would it be another sales call, or even worse thanks but no thanks.

'Hello this is a message for Abigail Williams. Tim Lambert here, we loved the scans of the watercolours you emailed us. You're what our advertising company needs. Care to meet up for an informal chat. Sorry to have missed you. We'll email you the details. Can't wait to hear from you.'

Abigail shook, she had to listen to the message again. Punching the air, she smiled. Goodbye Alessandro's. Hello new life.

The Forgotten War

The Forgotten War

by *Shura Price*

In the box I find a tiny handkerchief
like a folded leaf fraying,
a thin slip of lacquered air,
embroidered: a souvenir of France,
and a cut-throat razor.

Its tortoise-shell handle
sits in my palm,
a seductive curve
marking a storyline,
ready to splice, and carve
a tale to tell..

A Nazi badge, a photograph:
a girl, signed Nadia,
and Reichsbank notes,
funfzig mark Berlin 1914
zwanzigtausend mark 1923
kept folded neatly
next to
neat Union Jacks on pins.

Fragments of my parents' war,
smudged fingerprints
evidence of lost narrative
threads uncurling
lines unspoken,

The Forgotten War

Not a war of chic red on black solemnity
soothing, ordered formality,
well-rehearsed,
preserved in respectful silences,
just tangled half-truths,
secret illicit sympathies,
anger, hatred, pain
and
screaming sweated nightmares
drenched in guilt.

Better lost, forgotten, this private war.

Refold the notes, cut off the threads,
And close the lid.

Another Place

Another Place*

by *Les Marshall*

When we are made of iron
There will be no difference
Between land and sea
And our sightless eyes
Will shed no tears
Over words never spoken
Secure in our indifference
We shall not consider the Moon
Or fear the incoming tide
When we are made of iron

* Inspired by *Another Place* Sculpture by Anthony Gormley

Psycho-Active Strepsil

Psycho-Active Strepsil

by *Krishna Francis*

The concept for psycho active Strepsils had been mooted ten years previously. The idea was to create a sort of mental cough sweet for the timid to clear their metaphorical throats.

As with many good ideas the initial take up was slow. Even when the Glaxo Smith Klein began to develop it with serious intent the testing process was difficult to assess. Finding appropriate subjects proved hard. Teams of researchers put adverts in lonely hearts columns or on dating websites. It was felt that these places were teaming with subjects who might need help clearing the catarrh from their mental windpipes. A product like this would give them voice and help them express their desires clearly. Other places that were hunting grounds were in the backs of hobby magazines and on noticeboards in small branch line railway stations. The sorts of places that timid people might be looking, trainspotters and model aeroplane enthusiasts.

In the event it took for field agents to go out with clipboards. The problem of a blockage of this nature means that it is sometimes hard for sufferers to take advantage of what's on offer. Once small testing stations had been set up within selected localities it became easier. Likely looking test subjects often wearing bobble hats or crocs with socks were engaged in conversation on street corners and brought into the temporary research facility set up in a community centre or office space where a team of technicians ran them through

Psycho-Active Strepsil

a set of questions to assess their suitability and then handed out boxes of the sweets. They were given a questionnaire to fill in and sent on their way.

The return was surprising. Expecting limited responses a greater than usual number of subjects had been sought out. When over half of the subjects returned their answer sheets it was clear that a phenomena was growing.

Within a year of the television adverts coming into living rooms around the country there was a sea change in the general attitude of the nation. Quiet people who had gone about their business without much fuss suddenly began to make a noise about what they felt was going wrong in the world. The clearing of their mental passages had been so successful that they found they had something to say. More than just saying things clearly and with confidence for the first time, they were discovering a voice to express discontent. Boots rarely had stocks for longer than a week at a time as customers were consuming this wonder sweet at a furious rate. Local chemists formed cartels to get their hands on the product to give them a chance of competing with the large chains.

It all came to a head when the prime minister was doing a broadcast with his family around him. His son, a timid boy who had started taking the sweets on going to boarding school in order to cope with nerves began swearing at his father. He had been exposed to politics during history lessons. Finding that he couldn't stomach the politics his father voraciously expounded he wanted to speak up about them. One of the side effects that was warned about on the folded slip of paper that came with the box was seepage. Often involuntary utterances would be brought forth at inappropriate moments. Up until then the majority of cases had involved some entanglements with the authorities and a few upset teachers but that was all. In the aftermath of what was predictably called Strepsilgate all evidence of the product was removed from shelves and destroyed. Lobby groups were set up to protest but without the miracle sweet no-one could voice their concerns in suitably strong terms.

Seaside Town

in the Rain

Seaside Town in the Rain

by *Alison Shelton*

Dolls houses
huddled together
Unaffected by time
higgledy piggledy
jostling for space
on the hillsides.

Fishing boats
barnacle encrusted
seaweed roped
salt sprayed
jostling for space
in the swell

People
sunburned legs
bleached bodies
towel bearing
jostling for space
on the sand

Me and you
hand holding
jacket wearing
puddle jumping
All alone, together
in the rain

Indian Summer

by *Christine Potter*

Though clocks have gone back
daylight still comes early
the mist hangs low in the valley
a sheer veil rising with daybreak
over a millstone landscape

The day is festive, radiant with light
but with the menace of winter
a sharpness in shadow
and the early onset of evening
closing in on the day

Individual fallen leaves
glow orange, red, lime and rose
hardly mottled with death spots
spread across the pavements
like dabs of poster paints on dark tarmac

Enjoy the morning and noon
bask in the sun, it will not last long
hanging lower and lower in the sky
dazzling the unwary driver
but not the creeping dusk

Soon the unseasonable weather
will have been overwhelmed
warmth will come from the fireside
and the comfort of electricity, the cold
kept out behind drawn curtains.

Visit Me

by *Madeleine Cullinane*

There's the hoot of the taxi. Her friends are calling for her but Sarah takes a moment to look in the mirror one final time. It's Midsummer's eve, a night when the veils between this world and the other are at their thinnest. Sarah hardly registers her own reflection, instead she is focused on the room behind her, hoping his form will appear in the looking glass, wishing for his face to look over her shoulder and gaze into her eyes. But Sarah sees only her own pale painted features as she stands shivering in the flimsy gown of her elaborate fancy-dress.

Twenty minutes later the taxi is crunching up the driveway to the Hall. Sarah and her work-mates spill out, three fragrant Eighteenth century ladies as painted by Boucher, in Pompadour wigs and gowns of pastel taffeta decorated with satin bows and flounced Flemish lace.

The signage directs them through the wrought iron gates into the gardens where they show their tickets to the organiser's husband who is dressed as an embarrassed flunky. Sarah's friend Kate can't resist squeezing his turquoise-suited arm. 'It's not every guy who has the legs for knee-breeches,' she says. He is still beaming as he greets the next group of guests, enthusiastically offering them glittering overpriced masks on sticks. Sarah and her friends continue their progress around the house, giggling and rustling along the gravel paths between the box-edged flower beds of the formal knot garden.

When she was a young girl, a teenager, Sarah used to take risks. Now dressed in disguise for this masquerade ball she revels in that same feeling of hungry trepidation, her body yearning for excitement.

'Lovely to see you ladies. Complementary glass of champers?' says their hostess, the stoutest Marie Antoinette you could ever imagine. She indicates a table of drinks, they take it in turns to air kiss her cheek then with their faces masked the three friends glide off.

'It's fashionable to have a panel set into the front of your bodice,' says Sarah, behind her fan. 'But it looks like our hostess's gown has required extra panels at all four compass points.

The sounds of musicians tuning up in the ballroom come to them through the open French doors, whilst the aroma of roasting hog entices the party goers towards a marquee on the adjacent terrace. The paths leading from the gardens into the enchanted park beyond are lit by frosted solar ice rocks, and the trees on the fringe of the woods sparkle with waterproof fairy lights. No expense has been spared in the do-it-yourself store it seems.

Arm in arm with her companions Sarah strolls along sipping her Prosecco. Her senses are assaulted, she closes her eyes and conjures up Vauxhall Pleasure Gardens in its heyday on a hot summer's evening, the perfect setting for the spirits of the dead to mingle with the living. One glimpse of him would be enough, wouldn't it?

'Hello I'm Betty the fruit girl,' says the corporate wench. She offers them strawberries and cherries from her basket and directs them to the patio where their dining party are in sight. And what a sight their boss and colleagues make.

'Ah, here they are, the Three Graces,' says Sir at their approach. He has allotted himself the best view of the proceedings, thus with legs akimbo he sits at the head of the table ogling passing females and hailing fellow businessmen.

'Sir has gone the whole hog with his costume,' says Sarah's friend Jan.

'And the Macaroni wig suits him,' Sarah replies sotto voce. 'But the purple of his velvet suit shouts at the scarlet of his visage, and Sir's waistcoat buttons are strained ready for bursting.'

Pouring out a glass of wine from the cooler Sir pats the vacant gold chair beside him and Kate accepts his invitation, winking back at her friends. Sarah and Jan move down the table greeting colleagues until they find their places along with the office girls. The assembled company are a motley troupe of damsels and harlots, vagabonds and dandies with Saaed from accounts the only conscientious objector. He is lean and mean in his customary sharp suit, of silver-grey chambray on this occasion.

'Okay, I've settled my gown,' says Sarah. 'Now pour me a large glass of red.'

'And a white for me,' says Jan. 'Let's take full advantage of the boss's charity.'

Sarah is on glass number three and there is still no sign of dinner being served. Perhaps I should have had something to eat with the pills, she thinks, but bats away the reproaching voice. By time the food arrives Sarah has lost her appetite and just picks at her pork and apple sauce, then passes her cream filled profiteroles to Phoebe the pregnant one from reception. Sarah just has coffee and a mint.

You used to tell me to have confidence in myself, she thinks. I was your special girl and you would always look after me so now I challenge you to join me in celebrating at this feast. If your spirit is here somewhere why don't you show yourself?

Sarah cannot exactly recall them all trooping back indoors and relocating in the ballroom. It is unfortunate that the string quartet originally booked to perform at the event had to pull out at the last minute, but the swing band are good or at least enthusiastic, and it's a surreal treat to watch Eighteenth century couples attempting to dance the Lindy Hop.

'I can't sit still any longer,' says Jan. 'Come on let's dance, I haven't been to all those salsa classes for nothing.' Sarah suddenly comes to herself on the dance floor, where she is obliged to follow Jan's instructions, the swaying of her hips exaggerated by the panniers of her gown. 'Step forward one, two, then back...'

It is nearly midnight, the dynamics of the evening have changed as the guests intermingled or hived off. As she leaves the dance floor Sarah thinks she catches a fleeting glimpse of him from behind a pillar, or someone very like. She attempts to pursue him but somehow ends up back at her table where Sarah finds her friends are nowhere in sight and there is hardly anyone she chooses to sit with. Then she spots Phoebe's pink polyester gown; to accommodate her baby bump the young woman has opted for the roomy comfort of high-waisted mediaeval robe, with fake fur trim. Sarah catches her eye but Phoebe looks away, grimacing.

'Oh God Feebs, are you in pain, is it the baby?'

'No, well yes maybe. I need some air, but I don't want a fuss.' Sarah helps Phoebe out through the French doors onto the patio and to a carved stone seat in an alcove, then she phones the hospital. 'I'm sure everything will be fine,' says Sarah, conscious of her own thumping heart. 'It's such an auspicious night to welcome a new life into the world.' Phoebe grips her hand as together they listen to the whine of the ambulance and watch the blue light growing closer.

After she has handed Phoebe over to the paramedics Sarah is reluctant to go back inside and rejoin the revels. Instead she explores further into the gardens till the music and snatches of conversation have grown faint and Sarah finds herself on a romantic thoroughfare, a tree-lined avenue punctuated at regular intervals by floodlit Grecian statues, the highlights and shadows playing over their drapes and nudity.

Her thoughts return to him...it was such a shock, that first time. Afterwards it was like being born again in some-one else's body, though no-one seemed to notice that she was different, not even her mother. But it wasn't the end of the world, Sarah learned to tolerate his attentions, it meant he loved her.

Sarah comes to her senses, alarmed by shadowy figures that have appeared ahead of her; a group of hooded youths have eluded security and now obstruct her way. They move forward to surround her and one steps forward to grab her arm. Before Sarah can react the others take hold of her from all sides and her drawstring purse is dragged from her wrist.

'Let's get her into the bushes.'

'Oh no you don't, get your hands off her,' says the masked man who appears from nowhere. There is a scuffle then the youths run off. 'Are you hurt?' He turns back to her, and she thinks she recognises him.

'No, no, thanks, I'm fine,' she says, rubbing her sore wrist. 'And so relieved to see you.'

'They took your bag.' He bends to retrieve her lipstick from the gravel and returns it to her. 'Was there much else in it?'

'Just my phone and the money for the taxi home...'

His kiss silences her, she knows better than to struggle. On this night for remembering and honouring the dead he has come to her, she leans into his warmth, breathing in his aftershave and listening to his deep familiar voice resonating with her younger self. Afterwards she allows him to lead her back towards the lights and sounds of the party.

'There you are Sarah, come on the taxi is waiting!' Jan has found Sarah alone on the bench in the alcove with a twenty pound note crumpled in her hand. She gathers up her stained skirts and follows her friend through the house to the waiting car.

The Ballad of
Zaak and Ermaine

The Ballad of Zaak and Ermaine

by *Andy Fraser*

Part 1

You can live your life and love your love and think you are wise and urbane
But you'll never have heard, not a solitary word, about Zaak and his gentle Ermaine
For the doomed Ermaine didn't live above ground and nor did the terrible Zaak
So to be with them, you'll need a new rhythm, and rhymes that will work in the dark.

Down beneath your padding feet
Beneath your house, beneath the street
Down below the roots and stones
Past the boxes full of bones
Further still, beyond the drains
And whooshing of commuter trains
Down within that hoary gloom
There stands a dark and tragic tomb
Erected to a love in vain
Of poor Zaak and proud Ermaine

The Ballad of Zaak and Ermaine

Ermaine was a creature of noble stock and she held up her head with pride
For her family tree went back centuaries, with branches and stems on all sides
Her ears were floppy and eyes were large, though there was so little to see
She looked like a doe, but wore kimonos, which suited her admirably.

      And further still beneath the feet
      Of Ermaine's house on Ermaine's street
      Deeper down than mud and slime
      Back through rocks and back in time
      To caves and pools in darkness clear
      Where no light had ever peered
      There the white fish, blind as moles
      Swam in lakes as dark as coals
      And fishing on those glassy tops
      Lived the vicious Balamots

Zaak was not the most obvious choice, you wouldn't have called him a dish
He was slimy and squat; a Cave Balamot, and he lived on a diet of fish
Sunshine had never ventured this far and the caves were so dark decorated
But his back full of feathers could pinpoint wherever a sound had origionated.

The Ballad of Zaak and Ermaine

> They lived apart, quite unaware
> The other race was even there
> For aeons in their isolation
> Never one communication
> 'til one day the very rocks
> Above them shook with shaking shocks
> And with a terrifying sound
> A hole appeared in the ground
> Linking caves that never should
> Have been so linked, for bad or good.

The first to see this brand new world were the Balamot Fisherwife Maids
Who raised a petition for council decision on whether or not to invade
The motion was passed with a gnashing of teeth for an all-out, pre-emptive attack
And bravest amongst them, clad in green tungsten, set out the unfortunate Zaak

> They marched through caves of crystal hues
> Of golds and silvers, pinks and blues
> They marched past lakes of boiling rocks
> That burned their feet and singed their socks
> Up through chambers dry and bright
> Filled with sparkling stalactites
> And further still through forest gloom
> Of swaying fields of green mushroom
> 'til finally they came upon
> The fabled town of Yenis-Mon

The Ballad of Zaak and Ermaine

Now Queen Ermaine, ruled over this town as had her family before her
And public opinion throughout her dominion was everyone simply adored her.
But on the day when the Balamot came, all were so mighty distracted
For a crack in the ceiling had left them all feeling their very own lives had been fractured

>The fight was harsh, the battle quick
>Blood ran cold, and blood ran thick
>Through the gates they came in pairs
>And caught the guards quite unawares
>With flashing spear and dashing sword
>The Balamot army blindly poured.
>When Ermaine saw, alas too late,
>She met them to negotiate
>Through tears of pearl and heavy heart
>She spoke to battle-hardened, Zaak

Zaak was blind and couldn't see the beauty that stood supplicating
But still his keen hearing, found her endearing and utterly captiavating
And so she explained and he understood the extent of the Balamot blunder.
And the terrible Zaak, felt her words in his heart as if she would tear it asunder.

The Ballad of Zaak and Ermaine

> He heard how the attacks had come
> A-breaking rock and breaking bone
> From up above the heavens bright
> Above the stone, above the light
> And from these fissures water flowed
> To drip and crack and then explode
> Razing towns and lakes and all
> To bring an end to both their worlds
> And for the sake of future birth
> They vowed to heal the fractured earth.

Zaak was bold and volunteered, in remorse for the Balamot err
If Proud Ermaine would entertain his act of a true penitencer
Ermaine sighed and coyly said she would happily pardon each one
With just one condition, that on Zaak's great mission, she also would journey along.

> So, up amongst the rocks and streams
> Tied to ropes of glowing green
> Climbing up the watercourse
> Following toward its source
> Many days and nights they climbed
> Unaware of passing time
> Ever up they made their way
> Scaling shale and fractured clay
> Two figures clinging in the dark,
> Ermaine and her Erstwhile Zaak

Remembering David

Remembering David

by *Sue Silvester*

Ghostly echoes of a stranger's eulogy intertwined with Brahms' Lullaby, could not stop the numbness in my legs as a purple velvet curtain slowly closed upon my life. Words of condolence washed over my own private thoughts. David was gone.

It was raining lightly and neon lights blazed harshly red then green. The pulse of the city matched the ache in my head. A taxi cab waited as the sound of the rain became a whisper. 'Where to lady?' an oldish man with darting eyes and slightly balding grey hair rasped, tapping a gnarled finger on the steering wheel. 'Wolverhollow Bay,' I answered.

Dark factories loomed in the distance then faded into the background. Soon the city disappeared keeping unhappy memories concealed within. After an hour or so a golden beach came into view in a small horseshoe bay, the tide was on her way out leaving sand and small pebbles in its wake. A whitewashed house was standing alone. 'Pull in here,' I ordered and the taxi turned in to the driveway through wrought iron gates. Reaching into a black handbag, I produced a handful of notes, saying, 'Keep the change.'

Soon, entering alone through an old oak door, a musty smell hit my nostrils and dust covered the furniture. This was to be a sojourn, my home for now – away from the rat race and madding crowd. Purity filled my eardrums the sound of silence deafening. Soon to be alone, books and poetry were my only friends, solitude and the thoughts of David.

An old dusty record player beckoned from the corner of the room, lifting the lid a record still remained on the turntable. Pressing a black switch, the dulcet tones of a Jackie Wilson 1960s ballad burst into life. The opening bars sounded like Tchaikovsky, the title "Alone at Last" was so apt in my new world.

I never even made it to bed, falling into a deep sleep in an old black leather recliner; it had been a long day. For the next few weeks my mind constantly remembered my life with David. Endless summer holidays filled with sunshine, sometimes walking along the beach alone, his words whispered inside my brain. Seagulls danced above the waves lapping towards jagged rocks, salty spray cleansing my mind. Sometimes little things made me smile wistfully. I could almost feel his fingers lightly caressing my hair, the way rain nestled upon his cheeks. Little mannerisms and sayings played constantly in my head. David was the love of my life, now solitude is my one and only friend. Life must go on within me but without him.

A taxi cab screeched to a halt on my driveway stopping outside the old oak door, 'Where to lady?' Back to reality back to the rat race silent words shouted. 'Back to the city please.' Wolverhollow Bay disappeared into the distance. Dark factories loomed menacingly, it was raining lightly and neon lights blazed angrily as we entered the city limits. Life would never be the same for me again.

A Pleasure to Burn

A Pleasure to Burn

by *Christine Holley*

'It was a pleasure to burn, a special pleasure to see things eaten, to see things blackened and changed.'

But then that is how a barbecue should be, thought Tom, or at least if I am cooking. It was always his task to cook on these occasions even though in the kitchen pouring milk into a bowl of cereal was all he could do, and even then he might have to ask where the cereal was.

The golden rule, he told himself, was not to drink until at least some of the food had been despoiled. But, rules were made to be broken and while everyone else was furtively feeding sausages and burgers to the dog, he happily filled his glass time and again.

'What's that smell?' someone shouted, rather rudely Tom felt.

He couldn't detect anything unusual – burnt fat, smoke, dog flatulence – but then his nostrils, even though anaesthetised by copious amounts of alcohol, noticed something else. He looked down at the grid which should have been slowing destroying some pork chops – oh – somehow the plastic apron showing female genitalia had slipped off and landed on the barbecue and was slowly melting. He stepped back in alarm, this had not happened before, not even after a bottle of Cava, but the apron – now burning brightly - was still attached to him around the neck.

With uncharacteristic presence of mind he strode towards the frog pond, followed by barking dogs and delighted children who thought this was all part of the entertainment, along with inedible food and urinating in the bushes – and flung himself into the water. Decaying leaves, dead frogs rose to the surface giving off a pungent odour. Somehow Tom felt no urge to get up, but just lay there. Turning his head so he could breathe he saw with a grunt of satisfaction that in their attempt to douse the remains of the burning barbecue his guests had seized on what appeared to be a bottle of water and hurled the contents on the flames. His secret hoard of vodka caused the fire to shoot up into the air, removing eye brows and lashes on its way.

'How about a takeaway' said Tom, as they pulled him out of the pond.

There was a collective sigh of relief.

Late March and they are Still Not Here

Late March and they are Still Not Here

by *Shura Price*

Late March and they are still not here.
Sheets of hail slice the sky, cease,
leaving the air numb with cold.
The pond sits still, unoccupied,
no specks of life,
not a sign
of our
frogs.

A thin strip of fear flaps a warning.
A materialist, I fight, resist, and reject
words like omen, portent, sign, but
a needed pattern is broken,
a rhythm is interrupted;
I'm resentful at
familiarity fragmented,
disturbed.

Across the valley, a sunny school pond teems,
with slithering frogs, they orgy, wrestle, guarded
by circles of serious small children.
'Ours haven't come home.
Can I have some
of yours, please?'
Swift, fierce,
'No!'

Late March and they are Still Not Here

I recall a moment, a half thought, hesitation,
and pain pulls at my failure, picks
at my guilt like a scab:
a tiny frog lurching, trapped,
dying in deep snow,
while I watched,
last March.
Frozen.

Now, no splashes, no slippery eager bodies mating,
no joyful abandon in a sunlit pond,
no cushion of transparent blobs waiting
to wriggle into life, just
a dead still surface,
not a frog
not a
ripple.

Bombability

Bombability

by *Dan Clay*

Dr. Humphrey Fettle approached security sweating profusely underneath his white panama hat. Never a fan of the methane-like mugginess that predictably arose from mixing with other cabin cattle at 35,000 feet he had more reason that his irrational fear of flying to worry him today.

Placing his hand luggage, a newly-bought titanium briefcase, on the conveyor he slipped off his hat and jacket, noticing the damp patches under his arms seemed to be spreading further across his white shirt; something that momentarily distracted him from the call of the security officer on the other side of the detector gate.

'Sir, please make your way through,' it said; Humphrey keeping one eye on the case as it manoeuvred slowly along its journey like a coffin headed towards the certainty of fire.

Through he walked, metal and, for the moment, problem free and for a few seconds, before he saw the red light flash, the gaze of the lady behind the screen meet his and the arm of the guard a few feet away reach for his gun, he thought things might stay that way.

'Is that your case sir?' the voice asked sternly from behind the weapon's safety. Humphrey nodded. 'Would you mind telling me what's in it?'

'*What's in it?*' Humphrey thought, '*I think you bloody well know what's in it.*'

'A bomb, obviously,' he replied, registering the shock, surprise and fear that came over both the guard and the passengers around him, many of who he thought foolishly began fleeing for the exits. 'But don't worry, it's not going to go off!'

'Not very reassuring sir!' the guard snapped.

'Funny time to be making jokes,' Humphrey thought, having expected to be on the floor by now once caught, the odds of that ironically of course being much higher than those he was trying to beat.

'Why do you have a bomb in your case sir?' the guard continued, beginning to test Humphreys patience. He hadn't expected the average layman airport worker to understand complex mathematics, the kind he had been teaching to his university undergraduates that very afternoon, but he at least presumed he'd be allowed the chance to explain himself and be on his way.

'Safety,' he shouted, raising his eyes at the ignorance of the man.

'Sir?' the guard replied, dropping his weapon momentarily an inch or so in surprise.

'I'm a Professor of Statistics at Cambridge my good man, on his way to a conference in Zurich where I will be explaining how I took a bomb on a plane as an demonstration of a certain principle of probability.'

'What the fuck are you on Dr...Fettle?' the guard said, pausing slightly to register the name on the boarding card which lay sat in Humphrey's shirt pocket.

'Statistics show that the probability of a bomb being aboard an airplane is 1 in a 1,000. However the chance of two bombs being on the same plane rises to 1 in a million. Letting me take this bomb aboard will mean both I and the rest of the passengers aboard are much safer as a result,' he replied, noticing a smile emerge on the guard's face as he reached for his walky-talkie.

'Call the Bomb Squad,' he murmured into the device resting from his shoulder, 'and a shrink. We've got a right one here.'

Humphrey laughed. The exposure from this episode would as good as the keynote speech he was due to present tomorrow evening in all probability, cementing the very principle he was trying to demonstrate.

'Of course what you haven't calculated,' the guard began, moving his way towards Humphrey, lowering his gun as he approached closer, 'is that the second bomb doesn't negate the odds of the first, which still remain at 1 in a 1,000, which is roughly the chance you have of now leaving here with that smile still on your face.'

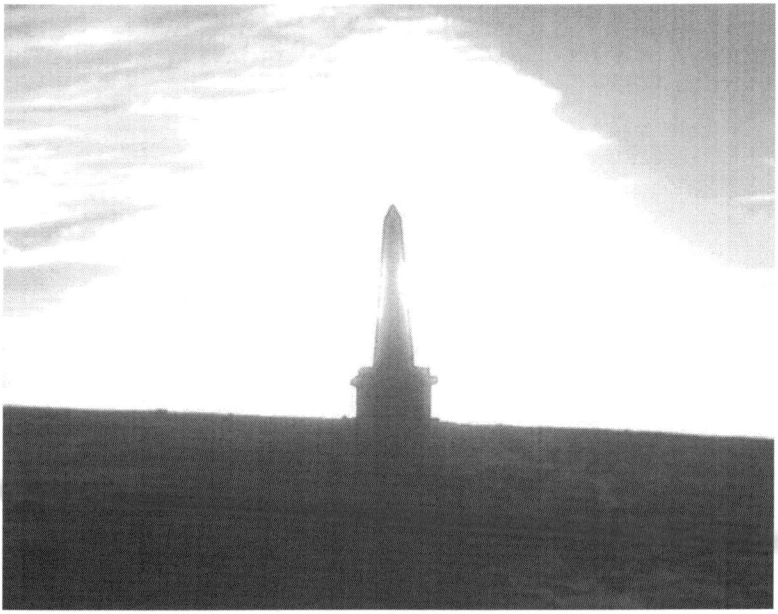

My Daughter's Breathing

My Daughter's Breathing

by *Anthony Peter*

My daughter's breathing. In the nightlight's softness
her little body acquaints itself with air to satisfy the
selving

she is held by, awake to all the orchards
scoped outside her mirador. But now, just two weeks
young, she breathes,

a Buddha in repose, pondering, perhaps,
the cradle of her mother's arms, the dreaming flesh she
pats,

the sweet curdling of its milk, the mystery
of her feet that feel the unwet, untrodden ocean of the air.

Her body's pod is working. She lets it
rise and fall, regulate itself in this her timeless world

that she's been clocked into; she hears her heartbeat,
feels the pulses of her blood that boost her hair, her nails,

that feed her liver, her lungs, her brain.
She is a matrix for the world's delights, sweet as a seed,

My Daughter's Breathing

bonny as a soft-shelled egg,
not yet helpless in her dreams, still embraced by this
room's unshadowy

womb-light. Her world's alive; she's shaping
all its shifts, its shimmerings, drawing in with all the
sense she can,

her breath of life. She's built on breath.
Breathe out, little girl, breathe in. Breathe out, breathe in.

The Working Dead

The Working Dead

A Trilogy by *Richard Holley*

The Good, The Dead and The Lucky

R can just make out the sound of the wind blowing through a single tree, he tries to isolate and focus on it completely in order to drown out the ambient sounds of modern life, and indeed, modern death.

The sun cannot be seen in the sky but R observes some beauty in a cumulonimbus cloud formation.

It is time.

R walks past the other job seekers, some groan in acknowledgement of his presence as flaps of their skin ripple in the wind, revealing putrefying flesh underneath, the myriad bandages wound around their wounds notwithstanding. Some reach out to grab at him, but R is unperturbed. Whilst the sight of such 'people' has become commonplace, society's more 'respectable' members find themselves disgusted by the sight, even deeply afeard. R is neither nauseous nor afraid. Is it because of a strong conviction? Most definitely not, even amongst the most depraved and lowly job seekers, one would be hard pressed to find anyone with less conviction than R. How is it then that R so easily glides amongst those that would inspire fear and revulsion within the hearts of society's more pious members?

One might observe that R is unable to recognise any meaningful difference between life and death. However, he is certainly not alone in that; an unfortunate consequence of a subtly post-apocalyptic society in the grip of an eschatological crisis where Hell no longer provides a convenient repository, mythological or otherwise, for the scum of the earth. Yet even if this wasn't the case, R would likely be as he is, for more so than anyone else in the North of England, past or present, R is simply unable to give a fuck about anything.

R sits down in front of Job Seeker coordinator.

'It's been 6 months now R; I'm afraid you are going to have to accept whatever job we offer you, look at this.' The coordinator slides an A4 sheet of paper detailing a job description. R observes it unenthusiastically.

'It's admin, I don't want to work in admin. Offices like that are full of zombies.'

'You're not allowed to say that, the accepted term is 'the necrotically gifted',' The coordinator says.

'You can't use necrosis as an adverb,' R says.

The coordinator stands, he is visibly infuriated, 'Oh listen to Mr English graduate, so well educated, but do you know what?'

'No he lived before my time,' R replies.

'Wwwwhat? Look I've had enough of your crap and your superior, cock sure, blase attitude, you're no better than those rotting bags of puss out there, you dole dossing scum! Well now it's payback. It's been six months which means I have the power to make you get a job, to make you just as miserable as me and if you refuse, I cut your money. From this day forth you can without any shadow of a doubt consider yourself to be my bitch!" The coordinator slumps into his chair and breathes a sigh of elated exultation, "God that felt good.'

'I appreciate your honesty and the frank and open fashion with which you have chosen to address me and since you have sold the job to me so well I would be delighted to accept your offer,' R says.

'And don't even think about quitting or getting yourself fired, not if you want to see your precious dole money again. I want you to remember me every time you look in a mirror or see your reflection as you vomit into a toilet filled with piss; remember me and how much I own your bitch ass." The coordinator breaks into a jubilant smile, "Now Fuck off!!'

R walks down the high street. He feels at one with the "necrotically gifted". The genetic refuse unceremoniously refused by respectable society who shuffle around moaning for 'brrrrraaaaiiiinnnnssss.'

'One advantage in such a world as this,' R says to himself, 'is that nobody cares anymore if you talk to yourself:

'An opportunity missed
A life ignored
Over 25 is too late to make a start
So join the army of the undead
And work the jobs that nobody wants

'When there is no room left in Hell
The Dead will work in admin
Give up your will to procedure
Because your soul will no longer matter
But at least 'The Good' will say you are lucky'

For a Few Corpses More

In the middle of the 21st Century, a mysterious virus was unleashed on the earth which caused the dead to rise from their graves. Unable to cope with the growing numbers of the undead, the government undertook a strategy to have the newly named, 'necrotically advantaged,' integrated back into society. This involved giving all of the "necrotically advantaged"

The Working Dead

jobs in the civil service and administration, alongside the 'living' (if indeed it is not too much of a stretch to describe an individual working in admin as 'alive').

'I suppose if I'm starting a job I might as well enjoy some of the associated perks...' R thought to himself the day before starting work. He spent the last of his dole money on 3 bottles of pinot grigio and a bottle of Wild Turkey Bourbon which he promptly consumed whilst listening to Wagner's Ring Cycle. R promised himself he would listen to the entirety of the opera in one sitting; he lasted 5 hours before collapsing into a pool of his own vomit.

The following morning, operating on autopilot, R stumbled from a train onto the station platform. Specks of rain fell from the grey clouds over head.

'It is a proper morning to fly into Hell,' the voice was that of a priest. Much like the undead, priests had become an increasingly common sight in Lancashire; the zombie apocalypse acting as a kind of January Sale for the Catholic Church who now found they could hook the remaining souls of the living at a steal.

'Is this Hell Father?' R enquired.

'Alas not my son, thou art... in ACCRINGTON!' The priest boomed and he pointed menacingly at R as thunder rumbled through the sky.

'Nooooooooooo!!!!' R howled.

Much of what followed was a blur to R until he arrived at the reception of his new job. R expected to be sent away, owing to his obviously hung over state, but the receptionist, believing R to be a zombie, steered him in the direction of the manager's office by jabbing at him with a the handle of a mop.

At an untidy desk in the office sat a large grey, cadaverous figure with a gaping mouth and a single pulsating eye.

'Even the manager is a zombie?' R thought out loud, 'Maybe this won't be so bad after all.'

The Working Dead

'Muttaugh, hack,' the manager spluttered, 'You must be R, huh, huh, huh, sent by the Jobcentre? I have lots of extremely tedious work for you to do.... GET BACK!' The manager blurted out, as he used his crutch to beat away some advancing zombies.

'Ok,' said R, 'Would you like me to clean the shit off your shoes, perhaps?'

'That is not necessary as yet,' The manager replied. 'Maybe after lunch time... Back I say, Get BACK!' The one eyed manager wheezed with fatigue from fighting off the zombies before again addressing R, 'There're a couple of bums down the corridor, they're dole rejects just like you; they will sort you out with some preliminary inspiration for suicide, huh, huh, huh.'

'Thank you, it has been a pleasure meeting you,' R said as he turned to leave.

'I see great promise in you R; I can see right now that you will become a loyal servant to the cause before your blood is even cold... BACK, GET BACK DAMN YOU!' The zombies had begun to overpower the manager, 'GET... LET GO OF ME...R! R! HELPPPP MEEEE!'

R was about to help the manager when a thought occurred to him: if the manager was dead, then R wouldn't have to do quite as much work. In light of this realisation R turned to leave with a big smile on his face.

'R, R, you'll burn in Hell, R!' The Manager gurgled as the zombies tore chunks of flesh from his arms and torso.

'Yes, it seems that way,' R observed nonchalantly, 'but as you of all people should know, "In the land of the blind; the one eyed man is king."'

'Fuck you R, you treacherous little cu...' R had exited the room and slammed the door before the manager could finish.

Employment rights meant that because of his years of service, the now undead manager was able to keep his job. With a zombie for a manager, R was completely free to

The Working Dead

procrastinate to his heart's content and so he lived happily ever after... well, as happy as the miserable wretch was capable of being.

A Fistful of Prozac

R joined followed the manager's directions to find a couple of similarly disillusioned vocational rejects sat in an office. One of them was hunched over his desk, sweat dripping from his brow. His eyes darted about, surveying the keyboard desperately as he ineffectually stabbed at the inexplicably placed characters with the index finger of each hand.

The other administrator was slouched in his chair and he slapped at the keyboard lazily, evidently out of a want of something else to do rather than a desire to do work. 'Aright mate," he said with little more than a passing glance at R, 'Have you ever fucked a zombie?' The administrator asked and he gestured at an undead filing clerk who looked up and smiled at R as a dark green sludge oozed from her mouth.

'Isn't that illegal?' R queried in as disaffected a tone as he could muster. It was council policy not to discriminate against sexual orientation and R did not want to start off on the wrong foot.

'All the Police from shit hole towns like this were reassigned to the important places, here we can do whatever we want, as long as you don't get caught by health and safety.'

'What about the bite?'

'Ah, you just wait till she goes for the bottom drawer and...' R shut his mind off from the unenlightening chatter of his colleague and surveyed the environment for the best skiving opportunities, he pondered this for several minutes, then realised his unashamedly deviant co-worker was still relating

The Working Dead

his myriad sordid escapades, 'I tell you, birds love it when you're circumcised; no purple headed warrior, no cheese...'

'Oh won't you just shut the fuck up!' The first administrator snapped. He stood to unleash a verbal tirade against the second administrator but was pacified by an arresting scent of jasmine. R for all his phlegmaticness was similarly affected and caught sight of a girl standing in the doorway looking right at him. She was not much younger than R but the calm gaze of her green eyes seemed beset with a synthetic wisdom born from years of madness overcome.

'Haven't seen you before,' The girl said, 'No sooner do I hear the boss has taken his rightful place in Hell than you appear. Could you finally be the one?'

'The one? I er, I'm not sure I follow.' R stammered.

'Do you want to?'

'Want to what?'

'Follow? Unless you'd rather stay and be a part of the edifying discourse of this room.'

'No, please lead the way.' R jumped up and moved close to the mysterious girl smelling of jasmine.

'My name is Ceri by the way; it is a Welsh name, I'm an outsider much, I imagine, like you.'

'I used to think I was,' R said, 'but the more the more dead people I see, the less I feel different.'

'No one actually knows what caused this. Imagine if you discovered that you were the cause; would you feel cursed or would you feel God had chosen you as his angel of death?'

'I don't think I'd feel anything.'

'Shall we find out?' Ceri opened a door into a room filled with guns, R's eyes lit up. 'Pick one,' Ceri said.

R grabbed an 1888 model repeater shotgun and an ammo belt, 'I've wanted one of these ever since I was 10 years old.'

'Let me guess; first time you saw Terminator 2?' Ceri said as she grabbed a pair of desert eagle pistols, 'It's my favourite movie too.'

The Working Dead

R was at a loss for words, he was smiling and realised it was the first time he had really smiled for longer than he cared to remember.

Ceri lead R to the outside of a large room.

'Are we going to clean up zombies?' R asked.

'I align myself with the belief that the undead are rightly or wrongly a part of this world. They are not the problem, the bureaucrats are the problem, besides zombies are cool, bureaucrats are most definitely not cool.'

'Here, here. So what is this room?'

'This is the department of health and safety and school inspections. Are you sure you are ready for this.'

'Hell yes,' R asserted as they kicked the doors open and proceeded to unload their weapons with frivolous impunity.

A stout balding fellow with a furrowed brow, pointy nose and veins popping out of his neck from the tightness of his tie approached R, 'I have to inform you, the decibel level of your activity contravenes article 13 of the Boredom Act, 1978'

'You have so got to die,' R said and attempted to shoot the waffling clerk but he had run out of ammo, meanwhile the clerk proceeded with his toneless lecturing, 'CERI!' R screamed in despair, 'Help, help me!' Ceri quickly came to R's aid, using her last bullet to silence R's torturer, 'Hasta la vista... jobsworth,' R said.

The two looked around at the carnage, Ceri blew the smoke from her desert eagle. 'Prozac, hah, it's for amateurs.'

'I guess they had it coming,' R declared and looked into Ceri's dazzling green eyes.

'We all have it coming kid,' Ceri added and they both knew that while not quite Terminator 2, Unforgiven was a close second for both of them and their lips met in a burning kiss of theatrical madness.

A Midsummer Night's Dream

A Midsummer Night's Dream

by *Alison Shelton*

It is the longest day;
The time between dusk and dawn as small as the memory
of a second.
The birds' songs continue uncertainly;
hesitant tweets at the listening stars
The clock stoically tones the hours uncaring of the season
The park jackdaws stride like hooded monks,
cleaning up the edible detritus of the day and
men toss and turn in their beds;
disturbed by the creeping daylight.

It is the shortest night.
The lonely moon drifts past midnight and onto the shining
horizon
The boundary between night and day brushed aside
With no care for the dark's perfect silence.
Sacred Steps transformed by time into a meaningless
waltz.
As long-haired figures dance airily
Through the monoliths' shadows and
men toss and turn in their beds
unnerved by something they've forgotten

It is the midsummer's eve
And the fairy folk wait in the places between
While their hearts grow cold like dew in midwinter
Waiting

A Pterodactyl Lacking Charity

A Pterodactyl Lacking Charity

by *Les Marshall*

I was looking through my window
Gazing over Lumbutts way
 Watching Ramblers rambling
And the Farmers making hay.

When all of a sudden I saw it,
What a sight to see!
A leathery flapping flying thing
And heading straight for me.

I shouted for my wife
Hey Mabel come and look
The strangest bird you'll ever see
It's bigger than a duck!

I had to say it looked right grand
As we watched it dip and soar
Transfixed and mystified
At Tod's own Dinosaur.

It had no beak, but lots of teeth
And a deep and frightening roar.
It did a swoop and looped the loop
And landed on the One Stop Store.

A Pterodactyl Lacking Charity

For a while it seemed content
It's energy all spent,
Sitting in its new found lair
Above the market square.

But then a thoughtful look
Appeared on its face
When it got a savoury whiff
Of haddock cod and plaice.

Its nostrils flared and sniffed
As it flew into the sky
A wicked gleam appeared
In each Jurassic eye.

Like a guided missile
It prepared a dreadful shock
Descending on the wet fish stall
And clearing out its stock.

The owner was amazed
Shook rigid to the core
In despair the man cried out
I'll come to Tod no more.

But the ancient creature
Didn't seem to care
It swallowed one last kipper
And then took to the air.

The shoppers screamed and shouted
And thought it quite a lark
As the pterodactyl headed
Westward to the Park.

A Pterodactyl Lacking Charity

A brass band competition
Was taking place that day
And many music lovers
Had come to hear them play.

The mayor was there
With his lady wife
Looking quite demure
Listening to the Tod Brass Band
Strike up an overture.

He sat there in the morning sun
His chain was shining bright
The hovering pterodactyl
Thought it quite a sight.

The flying avaricious beast
Saw this glistening thing
And thought 'I like the look of that
I'll have that mayoral bling.

Now when it came to diving
The pterodactyl was no novice
In one dramatic swoop
It grabbed his chain of office.

It seemed as though the creatures plan
Was well and truly hatched
part from one small snag –
The mayor was still attatched.

Into the summer sky
The Civic Head ascended
Looking down he cried
'flipping heck, my mayoral term has ended!

But his wife gave a cheery smile
And didn't take it hard
Shouting to her kidnapped spouse
'don't forget to send a card'.

Flying over Cornholme the
Creature gathered speed
Then turned right for Bradford
Where pterodactyls breed.

And so the creature disappeared
Never to be seen again
And neither was the mayor
Nor his golden chain.

The Race

The Race

by *Cindy Shanks*

'Race you, Dad,' I shriek.
footsteps, falter, feet scrape
along the gravel,
watching you run, far ahead,
the oak tree our finishing post.
Turning round, your grey eyes gleam
you hold out your hands, waiting.

'Race you, Dad,' I joke.
Your footsteps, faltering,
Far behind my stride,
the oak tree, my finishing post.
Glancing round at the distant figure
reaching towards me,
your papery skin creases into a smile.

'Race you, son,' I yell.
Zooming past your head start,
your chunky legs falter far behind;
memories linger, sharp edges,
the echo of an old man calling -
drowned out by a young child's voice,
'You won, Dada.'

The End

The Contributors

In alphabetical order

Dan Clay – Dan hasn't put pen to paper as much as he'd have liked due to changing nappies, *cooing* and *ahhhhing* and assembling nursery furniture. He has found time to tread the boards and hopes to build on this creativity by writing a series of books for babies having seen how a few basic words and pictures can get you published.

Madeleine Cullinane – Maddie grew up in the Hertfordshire village of Bushey Heath, but has lived up North since the seventies. Her favourite colour is blue, her favourite number is five, seafood is her favourite dinner but don't ask her to choose between all those grandsons.

Krishna Francis – Krishna has recently turned away from a life of film-making and taken up the pen, to write his autobiography through the lens of his parents exile from their home in South Africa. He also writes about fairy tale characters.

Contributors

Andy Fraser – Up until this year, Andy was a grounded middle-aged man who cared for the environment and rescued small, furry animals from certain peril. Now he has sold his soul to the capitalist devil and gnaws on fresh kitten paws while plotting the downfall of mankind in extremely unpleasant ways. Once that is done he will probably get back to doing some writing.

Christine Holley – Christine enjoys the company of her dog and her cat, and anyone else who doesn't argue with her. On good days she will go out and spend large sums of money on useless objects, on bad days she will sit indoors and drink heavily. This is how a good writer spends their time.

Richard Holley – Richard lives and works in Burnley for the Public Sector. He tends to write poems about his life and stories that feature mindless zombies and the end of the world, sticking closely to the adage "write what you know".

Les Marshall – Les was born in Littleborough, but lived most of his life in Todmorden. He has worked as a farmhand, textile printer, and social worker. He joined the Todmorden Writers' Group around three years ago and finds the stimulation and encouragement provided by the group invaluable.

Anthony Peter – Ant Peter continues to write for pleasure, but is still nowhere near finding an answer to the question 'What is the difference between a poet and a Poet?' Thankfully, that does not prevent him enjoying the "intolerable wrestle with words and meanings" and the occasional Nutty Brown ale in the company of like-minded people.

Christine Potter – Christine, now retired, taught English and History, She started to write alongside her pupils to encourage them. Her poems often what she calls her very ordinary childhood. She has several unpublished novels waiting for their hour of glory.

Shura Price – Shura gardens, reads, and drinks wine. When she feels guilty about enjoying retirement, she tries to scribble something meaningful to balance out the pleasure.

Cindy Shanks – Cindy has been a member of Todmorden Writers' Group since 2009 and enjoys meeting up with people who are passionate about writing and books. An avid reader, she wishes she could write like the authors she loves.

Contributors

Alison Shelton – Alison lives in Todmorden with her partner, her dog and an errant pet rabbit. Despite running her own business she still finds time to write and this year has focused more on poetry rather than her usual short stories. She loves the inspiration she finds while out walking.

Sue Silvester – Among Sue's many interests are reading, knitting and walking. She has been a member of the writers' group for five years and really enjoys the camaraderie of the group and likes meeting people with similar interests.

Cover art by Les Marshall
Bride Stones and *Stoodley Pike* photographs courtesy of Alison Shelton